For Anna, of course. And our lovely dads, John and Bill.
Adam & Charlotte Guillain

For my special dad, Chris, and my big little brother, Gavin.
For Sue and Alice.
Ada Grey

EGMONT
We bring stories to life

First published in Great Britain 2016 by Egmont UK Limited
The Yellow Building, 1 Nicholas Road, London W11 4AN

www.egmont.co.uk

Text copyright © Adam and Charlotte Guillain 2016
Illustrations copyright © Ada Grey 2016

The moral rights of the authors and illustrator have been asserted.

ISBN 978 1 4052 7749 5

CIP catalogue record for this title is available from the British Library.

School for Dads

Adam and Charlotte Guillain

Illustrated by
Ada Grey

EGMONT

At the end of a long school day,

Anna waited by the gate,

Along with other children

Whose dads were running late.

School
for Dads

Are you always late?

Do you forget to pack snacks?

Learn to be a better dad ...

"I'm sorry, Anna,"
gasped her dad.
"Please don't be too mad."
She told him, "I'll forgive you,
If you go to School for Dads."

Early the next morning,

Dad was shaken from his snooze.

"It's time for school!" said Anna,

"Quick, get dressed and find your shoes!"

Dad whizzed around like lightning,

While Anna got his snack,

And put it with his lunch box
In a bag upon his back.

Anna and her friends set off
And took their dads to school.

"Wheeeeeeeee! I love this!" cried one dad, "Scooters are so cool!"

Anna got her dad to class
And helped him find his peg.
Her dad looked rather sweet, she thought,
In shorts, with hairy legs.

"Work hard," Anna told her dad,
"And do the best you can."
"You sound just like a teacher," said Dad.

Anna cried,
"I am!"

"The first lesson is very hard,"
Anna warned the dads.
"It's called, What you must NEVER DO.
These things are VERY BAD.

Don't ignore us
when we're talking,
And stop looking
at your phone.

Don't watch the news,
come out and play —
It's no fun on our own.

When we're playing
at a friend's house,
Don't call out,
It's time to go!

And most of all, above all else,
Please never answer NO."

At break time, all the dads burst out,
"Yippeeeeeeee, it's time to play!"
"They're just like kids!" laughed Anna,
"In every single way."

"Can we play too?"
asked one boy,
As he stood there
looking sad.

Anna sighed, "We still have things to teach
To make them better dads."

The next lesson they taught was art,
With sticky tape and glue.

One dad cheered, "When we get home
Just think what we can do!"

The dads worked hard all morning
And were ready for their lunch . . .

But in the hall they soon became
A loud and rowdy bunch.

"I wouldn't mind some crisps," said Anna's dad,
"Or maybe sweets?"

"Nice try, Dad," laughed Anna,
"But those things are just for treats."

After lunchtime, Anna said,
"We hope that you agree,

To keep up with your sporty kids,
You need to do PE."

Some dads found it easy,
But others huffed and puffed.

"Keep it up," said Anna,
When one gasped, "That's enough!"

In assembly her dad moaned,
"My bottom hurts – it's just not fair!"

"We know," said Anna, sitting
On her comfy teacher's chair.

It was getting close to home time,
And the children had to say,

That it wasn't very easy
Being grown-ups for a day.

Anna thought about
her own dad,

And how sometimes
he was late.

But in so many other ways,
Her dad was really great.

"Let's celebrate our dads," she called out,
"Each and every one.

We should all stand up and show and tell
the good things they have done."

So the dads all got a sticker,
And they cheered,

"We passed

the test!"

Then Anna turned and hugged her dad
And whispered,